this coloring book
belongs to

....

pencil and marker swatch chart

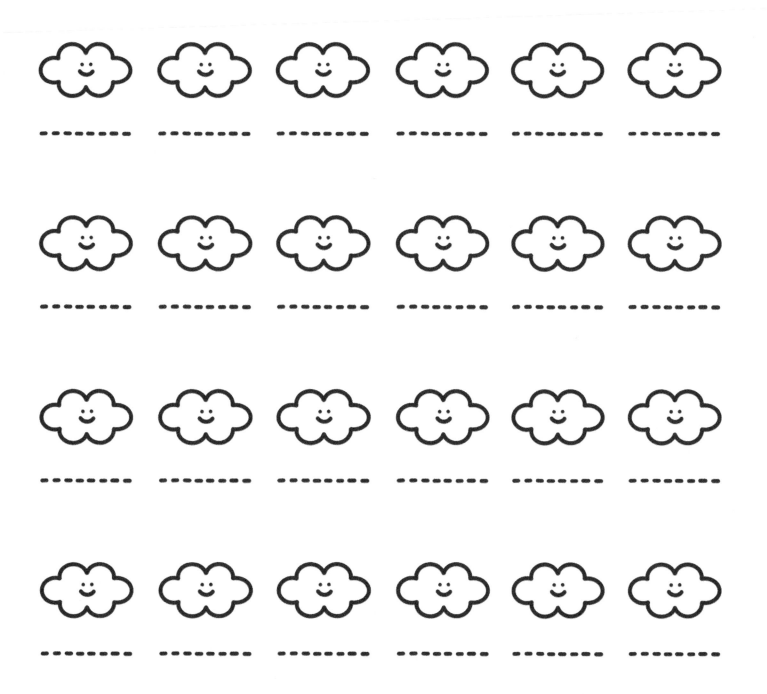

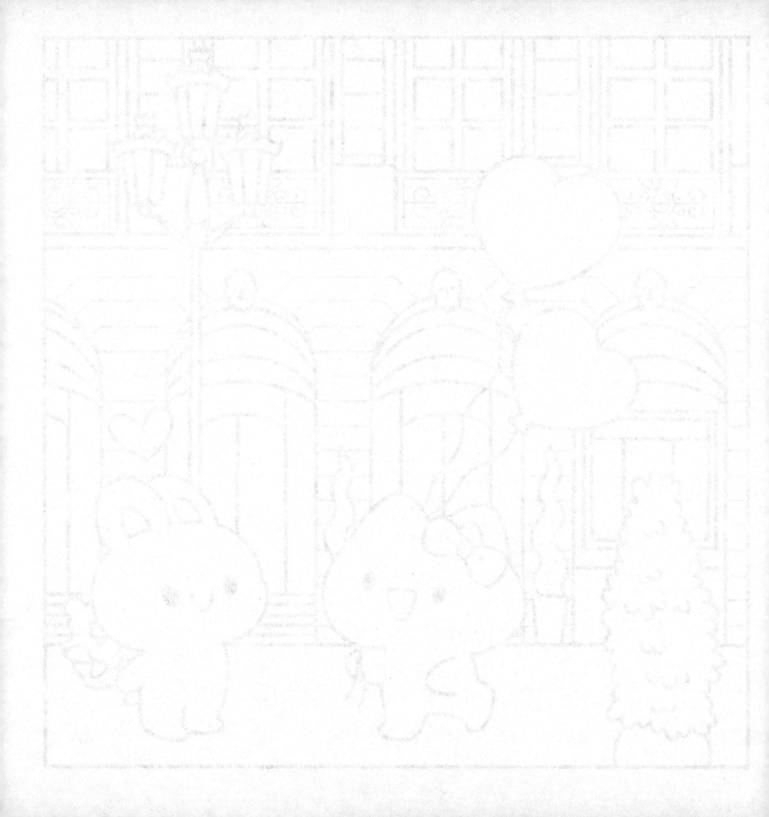

Your kawaii trip to Paris is complete! 🎉

But why stop here? Keep traveling with us by grabbing another cute destination from the Cool Kitsch Club! 🌸✈️

We love seeing your artwork, so tag us @theCoolKitschClub on Instagram and TikTok and share the love! 💕

If you enjoyed this adventure, leave us a review and help spread the cuteness!

Made in the USA
Monee, IL
11 December 2024

73178635R00050